TITCHY WITCH

AND THE BULLY BOGGARTS

ROSE IMPEY ★ KATHARINE McEWEN

ORCHARD

Titchy-witch

Victor

Eric

Wendel

Weeny-witch

Witchy-witch

Cat-a-bogus

Titchy-witch didn't want to go to school. She said she had a tummy-ache.

"Too many Grobble Gums," said Cat-a-bogus.

"All little witches have to go to school," said Mum.

"Even this little witch," said Dad.

Titchy-witch wanted Mum to take her to school, but Witchy-witch was too busy with the baby.

So Cat-a-bogus took her instead
and Titchy-witch scowled all
the way.

She didn't want anyone to see her
being taken to school by a cat!
But Gobby-goblin saw her.

When Titchy-witch stuck her nose in the air, the little goblin tripped her up.

So Titchy-witch turned his nose
into a sausage.

It soon turned back, but it still
made him mad.

Gobby-goblin's brother was a
terrible bully.
He stood on Titchy-witch's foot
and twisted her arm behind
her back.

So she turned his head into
a cabbage.

"You wait," said the cabbage.
"After school, we'll get our cousins
onto you. They're boggarts!"

But Titchy-witch didn't even wait
for Cat-a-bogus.
She set off home on her own.

When Titchy-witch was
half-way home, she heard a
whis-whis-whispering sound.

She knew what it was.
You could smell boggarts a mile
away.

Seven of them jumped out of the bushes. (Boggarts always travel in gangs. They're so stupid they'd get lost on their own.)

Titchy-witch wasn't afraid of one boggart. But seven!

The boggarts called her names:

And pulled her hair and pinched
her hat.

They tried to make Titchy-witch
cry, but even little witches
never cry.

"My dad will turn you all into toads," she said bravely.

"Let him," croaked the boggarts.

"My mum will turn you all into pigs," she said.

"Who cares," grunted the boggarts.

Then Titchy-witch had
a great idea.
She made up a spell:

"Pinch of sugar, pinch of spice.
All things pink and sweet and nice.
Turn these boggarts, brown and hairy,
Into little boggart-fairies."

The boggarts stared at each other
and started to squeal.

When they saw Cat-a-bogus
coming, the fairy-boggarts
ran away.

Cat-a-bogus told Titchy-witch she was getting too big for her broomstick.

He made her promise she would always wait for him from now on.

Cat-a-bogus was glad she'd learned her lesson, for once.

But Titchy-witch was planning
a little lesson of her own.

TITCHY WITCH

BY ROSE IMPEY ILLUSTRATED BY KATHARINE McEWEN

Enjoy a little more magic with all the Titchy-witch tales:

Orchard Books are available from all good
bookshops, or can be ordered from our website:
www.orchardbooks.co.uk
or telephone 01235 827702, or fax 01235 827703.

Prices and availability are subject to change.